the
song of the
chilɔRen of lír

Published by   De Vogel Ltd. 1983

Copyright © Michael Scott 1983
Illustrations © Rob C. Vogel 1983

ISBN: 0 946860 00 9

De Vogel Ltd., Skerries, Co. Dublin, Ireland

the song of the children of lir

De Vogel ltd.

For
Rebecca Devaney
and
Courtney Scott
both well worth waiting for.

We sing of a time
that is legend,
We speak of a race
that is myth,
We sing of the
Children of Lir.

Late in the afternoons, when the sun was just beginning to sink down behind the mountains in the west and the silver bell in the tiny church rang across the still waters of the lake, the children from the nearby town would gather around the ancient apple tree and listen to the small, pale woman in the long gown of woven brown wool.

She was no taller than the tallest one present, and yet she could never have been mistaken for one of them. Her face was round and smooth, unwrinkled, uncreased and pale — pale as the softest, whitest snow — and sometimes, when the sunlight touched her, the faintest tinge of green could be seen in her long flowing hair.

Her name was Fionuala, and she was one of the legendary Children of Lir.

When the children had gathered and arranged themselves in a semi-circle around her, she would lean back against the rough bark of the apple tree and in her low musical voice, tell them of her life and adventures in a time that had long since passed, a time of myth and legend, of sorcery and magic: the Age of the Tuatha De Danann.

Chapter

I

"When I was young," Fionuala began, "the world was a different, more magical place. Creatures and animals that are no longer alive now lived then; there were dragons in the air, monsters in the sea, and silver-horned unicorns ran in the forests. Magic still worked, and it worked because people believed that it worked. Nowadays, nobody believes in magic and its power is sadly diminished.

"My father was called Lir, and he was the Lord of the Sea. He was one of the ancient Tuatha De Danann, the People of the Goddess Danu, and they had conquered this land and taken it from the savage Fir Bolga. My mother was called Eva, who was also from the De Danann tribe and, like all the women of that tribe, she was very beautiful.

"At that time I had one brother, and my story properly begins on that day when Aed — for that was his name — and I were swimming . . ."

13

THE SONG OF THE CHILDREN OF LIR

The young boy and girl dived into the ice-cold water together and struck out strongly towards the far bank of the small lake. They did not swim like humans, who splashed and crashed noisily across the surface, for they folded their arms by their sides and used their slightly-webbed toes to push them along just beneath the surface of the lake. Nor did they need to hold their breaths, for they had a tiny set of fish-like gills set into the sides of their throats which allowed them to breathe under water.

And they were not like normal children, for Fionuála and Aed were the children of Lir, the Lord of the Sea and ruler of the *Tir faoi Thuinn,* the Land Beneath the Waves, and the children were equally at home on land or in the water.

When they reached the far side of the lake their heads broke the surface at the same time and they rose from the water up onto the grassy bank in one smooth leap, like salmon leaping over a weir. They stood in the shade of the weeping willows and shook themselves dry and Fionuala shook her hair loose and allowed the gentle breeze to blow it dry.

It would have been hard for a stranger to tell brother and sister apart for, both in looks, height and colouring they so resembled one another that they might have been taken for twins. The only distinguishing feature was that Fionuala's hair was slightly longer and thicker than her brother's, and it had a darker greenish tinge to it.

There was a sudden crashing in the woods behind them and they both leaped to the water's edge, ready to dive to safety beneath its icy waters if necessary. Although they were close to their father's Fort, wild beasts still managed to wander past the guards and occasionally bandits crept past them to raid the villages and scattered farms.

A twig snapped and then a huge figure in bronze armour brushed aside the branches and stepped into the glade. Fionuala and Aed both relaxed: it was one of their father's guards. He was red-faced and out-of-breath, for the day was very warm and he had run down from the Fort in his heavy armour.

"Your . . . your father, the king . . . wishes . . . wishes you to return . . . to the Fort . . . immediately," he gasped, leaning on his long spear while he caught his breath.

The two children thanked him and, dressing quickly in their green and gold tunics, they set off at a run for the White Fort. They slipped in and out of the bushes without disturbing a leaf, leaped across the many tiny streamlets without breaking step and vaulted over a fallen tree. However, as soon as they left the small wood they had to slow down, for the sun was now behind them and was reflecting off the polished stones and golden roof of the White Fort. The light was blinding and so, instead of climbing the hill to the main gate, they followed a side path around behind the Fort so that they were out of the glare and could race again.

They burst through the kitchen door side-by-side, both shouting that they had won . . . and then they stopped in shock. Mairid, the fat, old cook and Fodhla, one of their mother's maids were sitting by the huge, white-sanded table, crying. Before they could ask any questions, the heavy wooden door at the far end of the room opened and Mechar, their father's servant appeared. He stopped when he saw them and beckoned them forward.

He was a tall, powerfully-built man and, although he always seemed stern and forbidding, he treated the children as if they were his own. Without saying a word, he took them both by the hand and led them through corridors which were strangely empty at this time of day, although they should have been bustling with servants and guards.

"What's wrong, Mechar?" Fionuala asked quietly, suddenly frightened by his strange behaviour and the empty hallways. But he only shook his head and smiled sadly, and would say nothing.

He brought them down a corridor which led to a part of the Fort they had never been in before. It was dark and dim and there was a strong smell of seaweed and salt air about it. The walls of the corridor were not white, polished and sparkling like those in the rest of the Fort, but rather they were dark and stained, and there was a green fungus growing in the cracks between the stones. There were torches set into rusted brackets high on the walls, but they did little to light the way and only added to the strange mixture of smells.

Mechar stopped before a huge wooden door, and tapped gently on it with his fingertips in a strange rhythm. He then whispered a word and the door slowly creaked open. He then stood back and pushed the children gently forward. "You must go in yourselves," he said quietly.

Fionuala and Aed took a step forward into the room and immediately the door clicked shut behind them. However, they barely noticed it happening, for they were looking around in amazement. After the dark, dingy corridor, they had expected the room to be much the same, but instead it was sparkling, bright and clean. It was circular in shape and the walls, floor and ceiling were painted in varying shades of blue. Pictures of sea-creatures had been painted in perfect detail and in glowing colours onto the walls, and where the walls joined the floor there were more pictures, but this time of sea plants with long waving fronds, multi-coloured flowers and vividly coloured crabs and lobsters.

For a brief moment both children were fooled into thinking that they were under water and they felt the cold rush of air down their throats as their gills opened.

They took a few steps forward, looking around in wonder; they never suspected such a room existed in their own house.

A door opened in the wall just in front of them, and blue-green light streamed out. A tall figure stepped into the doorway, spread its arms and immediately the light died. Fionuala and Aed hung back uncertainly until the figure stepped out of the darkened doorway into the room and they recognized their father.

Lir was a huge man, standing taller than most of the other De Danann. In looks, he most resembled Fionuala, although his features were less rounded and harder, and the green tinge in his short, square-cut hair and beard was

17

very obvious. His skin was also touched with green and the webbing between his fingers and toes was more noticeable than his children's. He was dressed in a short, knee-length tunic of silver and emerald, and there were rings and bracelets of purest coral around his wrists.

"My children," he said quietly and stooped down to pick them both up, one in each arm.

"What is this place?" Aed asked, his eyes wide in astonishment.

Lir, the Lord of the Sea, smiled sadly. "This is a room I had hoped you would never have to see. This is the place where the people of our race go when they feel that they are near to their time for resting. There is a room like this in every Fort."

"What is *resting*, Father?" Aed asked.

"The human people would call it death, " Lir said slowly.

"But Father," Aed said in horror, "we are De Danann, we are immortal."

Lir nodded his great head and his grey-green eyes clouded with tears. "Although we may be immortal, little Aed, we need to rest for very long periods of time — sometimes lasting thousands of years or more! I suppose you might say it is a sort of death."

"Father," Fionuala asked, her voice little more than a whisper, "is it mother?"

Their father nodded briefly and then he put them down onto the polished stone floor again and, taking them both by the hand, led them into the second room.

It was smaller than the first, but painted in the same shades of blue, and the only piece of furniture in it was a long low bed of cream-coloured stone inset with sparkling shells. On the bed lay their mother Eva, dressed in her finest robe of pure pale green silk. Her eyes were closed and she looked as if she were sleeping.

"Here she will stay until she wakes," Lir said softly. "But she will be watching over you; she told me so before she slept, and if, at any time in the future, you are ever in any great danger, you need only call upon her, and she will be there." He released their hands and urged them forward. "You may kiss her for the last time."

Fionuala took Aed's hand and together they walked to the side of their mother's bed and kissed her on the cheek. It was hard to believe that she was gone from them forever, for she looked as if she might wake up at any moment.

Lir came and took them from the small blue room and when he closed the door, he whispered a word and immediately the opening disappeared and became part of the wall. He turned to the two children. "Before your mother came down to this room, she gave birth to twins, boys, and she wished that they would be called Fiac and Con." The tall king leaned down and kissed them both on the forehead. "Go now and see your brothers. Fionuala," he added gently, "you must be a mother to them both, and Aed," he looked at his son, "you must be their protector."

Chapter
II

"And so the years passed," Fionuala said, *"and my two little brothers grew up and oh, were they wild! Aed and I often found them climbing the walls of the Fort, or eating the unripened apples off the trees and they often went swimming in the rushing rivers that bordered our father's country. We had our hands full with them.*

"After our mother slept, our father changed. He was not the smiling, laughing man he used to be; he was often away in his Kingdom Beneath the Waves, and he took little or no interest in the White Fort. I did the best I could, but it was a huge rambling place and it soon began to look run-down and deserted, with the white walls unpolished and the golden roof tarnished and streaked.

"We spent a lot of time at our grandfather's Fort on the banks of Lough Derg and the River Shannon. He was called Bov Dearg or Red Bov, because of his fiery red hair and beard, and at that time he was king of all Banba, as Ireland was called in those days.

"Now, the year that I was sixteen, Aed fifteen and Fiac and Con six, we spent most of the summer with him. When our holiday was over a company of warriors led by Mechar would usually come to escort us home, but this time our father himself came to collect us. And it was then he met Aife, our mother's sister . . ."

Aife was beautiful. Even the women of the Tuatha De Danann, who were amongst the most beautiful in the world, had to acknowledge that she was the most beautiful of all.

She was very tall — as tall as her father, Bov — and her face was almost heart-shaped and came to a pointed chin. Her ears too, were slightly pointed and her green eyes slanted upwards a little. But her loveliest feature was her hair, which was as black as soot and flowed down to her knees in a long shimmering cloak. What made it all the more unusual and startling were the two bands of dark green hair that started just above her ears and rippled half-way down her flowing hair.

Perhaps it was her looks that first attracted Lir to her, or maybe it was her resemblance to her sister, for in many respects they were quite similar. Lir stayed at Bov's Fort for several weeks and spent most of the time in Aife's company. They went hunting and fishing together in the huge forests that surrounded the Fort. They took the four children for

23

picnics by the banks of the mighty Shannon, or they would borrow a boat and row out across Lough Derg and watch the setting sun turn the waters the colour of bright shimmering gold.

On one occasion when they were out boating on the lake, a sudden storm blew up and they were forced to take shelter on one of the tiny islands that were scattered through the water. To pass the time Aife showed the children some of her magic. She had Con fetch her a handful of sand and asked him what he would like her to turn it into.

"Turn it into gold," Con said eagerly.

Aife smiled and covered Con's tiny hand with her own, equally small fingers. She closed her eyes and her lips moved in the strange musical speech of the ancient Tuatha De Danann, a language that the younger people could barely

speak. Immediately, a bright greenish glow spread from her fingertips, and Con began to giggle because he said it felt as if he were being tickled. Aife stopped her low crooning and the greenish glow died; she then tipped his closed hands once with her long, pointed nails and then she asked him to open his hands. When he did he found he was holding a handful of bright gold instead of worthless sand.

Aife turned to Fiac. "And what would you like me to do?"

The young boy stooped and picked up a large pebble. "Can you make it into a diamond?" he asked slowly and carefully, for he tended to stutter when he grew excited.

Aife took the pebble and cupped her hands around it. She then bent over and breathed on it and Fionuala and her father leaned forward to watch her. They saw the stone begin to change colour, the rough greyness slowly disappearing to be replaced with a pale milky colour, which in turn changed to a crystal clearness. Aife smiled and held up the large, pure diamond between her finger and thumb.

She then looked at Aed and he handed her a stick and asked her to make it into a sword for him. She took the branch and pressed it down into the soft sand until it was completely covered. With her long pointed nails she traced out strange symbols and patterns onto the sand, and then

she whispered a *word*. Immediately the countless grains of sand began to move of their own accord, and the children watched fascinated as the shifting patterns almost spelt words in the De Danann language. The sands shifted and turned one last time, and then stopped. Aife carefully uncovered the stick with her small, delicate hands, and then she withdrew a short, gleaming metal sword with a bronze hilt from the ground.

Aife then turned to Fionuala. "And what would you have me do?" she asked gently.

The young girl carefully parted a leaf on the bush by her side and, with infinite care, she handed over a tiny, fuzzy caterpiller. "Can you change this into a butterfly?" she asked.

Her aunt took the tiny wriggling creature onto her finger, breathed once onto it and then tossed it up into the air! Lir and the four children clearly saw a silky cocoon appear around the creature, fall off almost immediately, and a bright black and yellow butterfly appear. It fluttered once or twice, testing its wings, and then it drifted down and rested on Fionuala's arm, its tissue-like wings still damp and beating gently.

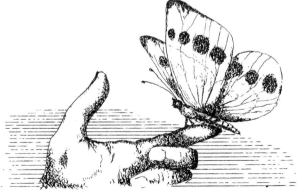

"How can you do that?" Fionuala asked in a whisper.

"My power is that of transformation," Aife explained. "I can change things, small things usually, but if I had my magical cloak, I could change that lake into milk, and the distant mountains into glass."

Fionuala shivered. "That's a frightening power," she said.

Her aunt shrugged. "Oh, mine is only a small talent; my father is a far stronger magician and sorcerer than I will ever be."

Lir stood up, rubbing his hands against his back, which had gone stiff from sitting in the one position for so long. "Look, the storm is dying down," he said. "We might as well head back to your grandfather's Fort."

"But it's so far away," Aed complained, "and I don't feel like rowing."

"Well, if you get into the boat," Lir said, "I'll show you a little magic of my own." And, when they were all safely seated in the small round boat, Lir dipped his hand in the water and moved his fingers to and fro in a strange way. There was a sudden swelling in the calm waters and a strong wave formed beneath the boat and carried it swiftly and smoothly to the far shore.

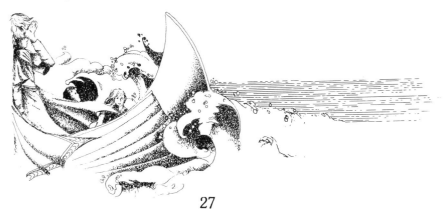

Lir and Aife married a short while later, and the wedding ceremony, conducted in the old-fashioned way in the midst of a forest, was attended by nearly all the lords and ladies of the Tuatha De Danann.

Fionuala was her aunt's bridesmaid, whilst Fiac and Con carried the train of her long shimmering silver gown, and Aed walked before her, carrying his father's coral sword.

When the ceremony had been completed and the couple had been blessed by the white-robed priest, the guests went back to Bov's Fort, where there was feasting and dancing until the day turned to shadow and night crept in from the east and one by one the night stars appeared in the purple sky.

There were singers, dancers and jugglers, and then a bard came and sat by the huge open fire, and he told the stories of the stars, picking them out one by one and explaining how they had come by their names and found their ways into the heavens.

But the day had been long and tiring and even though they found his stories fascinating, the children of Lir nodded off and fell asleep, and that night, their dreams were strange and peaceful.

III

"And so we returned to the White Fort with our new step-mother, and she set about making the Fort a place to live in once again.

"She ordered the white walls painted in bright new paint that one of the old women in the village made from the bark of certain trees and the berries off the bushes. She gave instructions for the roof to be cleaned and twenty men, with their helpers, worked for more than twenty days just cleaning the gold tiles, digging out the tufts of grass that had taken root there, and cleaning off the white streaks left by the birds.

"In those early days, Aife was kind and gentle to us and treated us as if we were her own children. However, as the months passed, she began to change towards us. At first it was just in little ways; things we would do or say would anger her for no reason, and I sometimes found her looking at us in a strange way, in a way that frightened me.

"I can remember that last summer very clearly . . ."

Fionuala stood beneath the apple tree with Fiac and Con by her side. They were watching Aed who was up in the very highest branches of the tree, carefully unravelling Con's kite which had become entangled in the branches.

"Be careful," Fionuala said quietly, afraid that a shout might startle her brother and cause him to fall.

"Yes," Con added, "it's a new kite and I don't want it torn or damaged."

Aed laughed and dropped a small unripened apple down on his brother's head. He pulled another free and was just about to drop it, when he stopped and the laughter froze in his throat. His brothers and sister followed the direction of his gaze and turned around. Aife was approaching. When Fionuala saw who it was, she started to smile and half-raised her hand in greeting, but then she stopped when she saw the expression on her step-mother's face. Con took hold of his sister's hand with fright, for Aife's expression was frightening to look upon.

She strode through the little orchard along the muddy path, her high, doe-skin boots sinking into the soft earth, and the hem of her long gown trailing in the muck. She stopped about five paces from the children. She was shivering with rage and made two attempts to speak before her voice came out without trembling.

"Just what do you think you are doing?" she demanded coldly.

"Why, nothing . . ." Aed began.

"Nothing!" she snapped. "Nothing. I told you before not to come into this orchard again; you have been warned about climbing trees, and yet here you are, openly defying me. And not only that, but you're also destroying the fruit."

"I only climbed up to get . . ." Aed started to say, but Aife cut him short.

"I will not listen to any excuses. You can all return to your rooms, and I do not want to see you again before tomorrow morning."

"But supper . . ." Fiac said quietly.

"You should have thought of that before!" Aife snapped and, turning on her heel, marched back along the path towards the Fort.

The four children watched her disappear and then Fiac began to cry softly. Fionuala held and comforted him, although she very much felt like crying herself; it was so unfair, they weren't doing anything wrong.

Aed freed Con's kite and lowered it down to him by the tangled string, and then they set out for the Fort along a different route to the one their step-mother had taken, one which would take them in by the kitchens.

On their way through the kitchen gardens, they met Mechar, their father's servant. He stopped when he saw their woeful expressions. Stooping down, he lifted up both Con and Fiac in his strong arms. "What's the matter with you, eh?" he asked, his usually harsh voice soft and concerned.

"Our step-mother spoke harshly to us," Con said quietly.

"And . . . and for no reason," his brother added, with a slight stammer, "we . . . we were doing nothing."

Fionuala nodded. "She did seem a little upset."

Mechar's expression changed and he put the twins down slowly. "Why don't you run along into the kitchen," he suggested, "I think Mairid made some honey-and-nut cakes earlier on."

"Honey-and-nut . . ."

"Our favourites . . ."

And they were gone, racing down the path towards the kitchen door, their upset already forgotten.

Mechar watched them go with a slight smile on his lips, and then he turned back to the two older children. "Why don't we walk in the garden," he said softly.

Aed and Fionuala followed the tall figure out into the small garden that was set apart from the kitchen and herb gardens by a high wall. It had been their mother's private garden and her special pride and joy, and she used to spend many afternoons tending to the trees and flowers that travellers brought to her from the four corners of the world. In the height of summer it was usually a mass of living colour and you could taste the many strange scents on the air.

But now however, at the time when everything should have been in full bloom, it was overrun with weeds and nettles, and tall grasses grew between the ornamental flower-beds and choked the little stream and artificial lake.

Fionuala felt tears sting her eyes when she remembered how carefully her mother had kept this little garden, and how disappointed she would be if she saw how badly kept it was now. Of course, Aife had no interest in flowers and gardening.

Mechar led them along a path overgrown with weeds and brambles. A small tree had fallen across their path and they had to detour around it to reach the tiny lake.

35

Mechar stopped by the side of the still water, his head bowed and his hands buried in his large sleeves.

"I have been with your father for many years," he said suddenly, startling them both. "I was by his side when we sailed on our ships of metal and magic from the cities in the north to this green and fertile land." He smiled suddenly, "And you might not know this, but he and I are cousins of sorts, and I suppose that would make us relations of a distant kind." He turned around and stood with his back to the water. "I have always thought of you as my own children and, if I have ever been harsh with you, it was only to keep you from harm. But now children I am frightened. Oh, not for myself, but for you!"

"But why, Mechar?" Fionuala asked in a whisper.

"This has something to do with our step-mother, hasn't it?" Aed asked.

Mechar nodded. "Your step-mother went to see the wise woman in the village today," he began. "She asked the old witch would she ever bear your father any children, and the answer was no."

Mechar saw their looks of puzzlement and continued. "You see, according to the law, the four of you — the children of Lir — will inherit your father's land and fortune when he decides to abdicate or the long sleep takes him. However, if Aife were to have a child, then that child would be the sole heir, and you would get nothing."

"And Aife was told she would never bear any children," Aed said, "it's no wonder she was so angry."

"It's very sad that she should be childless," Fionuala said, "but she does have us; and why should that make you frightened for us?"

"I fear that since she can have no children of her own, she might just decide that there should be no children at all to inherit!"

Aed and Fionuala looked at him in horror; what he was suggesting was . . . impossible.

"But we are De Danann, we cannot be killed!" Aed protested.

Mechar shook his head. "Of course you can be killed. But what would happen is that your ghost would not rest until your murderer had been caught and punished. But you would be very much dead, I'm afraid."

Fionuala, who had pulled a dead leaf off a tree and had been twirling it between her fingers, suddenly threw the remains onto the green-scummed water. "But surely that would prevent her from killing us. I mean, she knows that she would be found out."

"But she could always have you kidnapped and taken to the four corners of the world," Mechar said quickly. "All I'm asking you to do is to be extra careful, especially when your step-mother is around. Promise me?" he asked tensely.

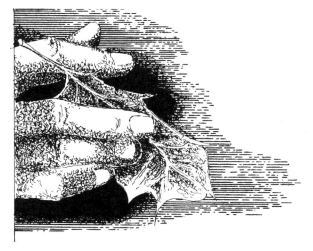

A little frightened by his obvious concern, they both nodded their heads.

Mechar then reached into the pouch that he carried on his belt and pulled out two small black stones. There was a small circular hole through the centre of each stone, and a leather thong looped through it. He hung the stones around the children's necks by the thongs.

"You must promise me that you will wear these always," he insisted. "These are the Stones of Truth; they are older than the Tuatha De Danann, and are touched with the First Magic ever to come into this world. Wear them and I will always know where to find you." The tall man smiled briefly and then turned and made his way back through the overgrown garden towards the kitchens.

Aed and Fionuala stood and watched him disappear through the trees, and when he was gone they turned back and stared into the still green waters of the stagnant lake, and then they both suddenly shivered, although it was not a cold evening . . .

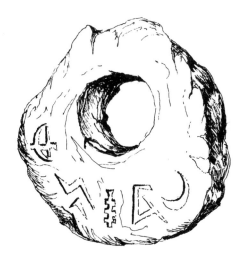

Chapter
IV

"Our step-mother's attitude changed towards us from that day. We could do nothing right, everything we did was wrong and she said that we did it just to annoy her.

"We were no longer allowed to go swimming in the lakes and streams; no longer allowed to climb the trees or wander along the corridors of our father's Fort, and we were forbidden to go into the gardens.

"She often spoke to our father about us, but he loved us very deeply and would hear nothing bad said about us. And Aife hated us all the more for this, and I suppose she believed that he loved us more than he loved her – which was not true: he loved her very deeply.

"Aife then fell ill – or she claimed that she fell ill – for when our father sent the best doctors and wizards to her, they could all find nothing wrong with her, and said that it was a sickness of the mind rather than of the body.

"Aife however, insisted that she was sick, and so she kept to her bed. She refused to see us, for she claimed that we made her feel worse, and she rarely saw our father. She spent a whole year in bed!

"And then, one day when our father was away with his men hunting down a wild boar that was destroying the crops and killing the farm animals, Aife 'recovered' . . ."

A sudden silence greeted Aife's appearance in the courtyard of the White Fort. The Queen hadn't been seen in over a year; she was supposed to be dreadfully ill and close to death — true death, that is, and not the long-lasting sleep of the De Danann.

Fionuala and Aed looked up as the tall shadow fell across them. They were sitting on one of the lower steps playing a board game with twigs and stones, moving the pieces to and fro, winning and losing them again. When they saw their step-mother, they both hurriedly scrambled to their feet, their game forgotten.

A year in bed had changed her. For a start she had put on a lot of weight, and her lovely face had grown puffy, and there were now bags under her eyes. There were fine threads of silver and grey in her hair, which was no longer as thick and shining as it had once been.

Aed was the first to recover from the shock of seeing his step-mother. "My lady . . . are you well?" he asked quickly.

"I am somewhat recovered, thank you" Aife said coldly, and her thin lips moved in a quick, icy smile.

"Has your illness passed?" Fionuala asked.

Aife came slowly down the steps, casually kicking their board game out of her way. "It has gone for a little time, I think." She smiled again. "However, I think I shall soon be rid of it forever," she added in a strange voice, and this time her smile was frightening. She walked past the children and out into the centre of the small courtyard, and then she stopped and looked back over her shoulder. "I found I could not stay in bed on this lovely day. I think it would be the perfect day to visit your grandfather," she said. "We can bring a picnic with us. What do you think?" Without waiting for an answer, she turned away and strode across the courtyard, calling for the servants to prepare her chariot and to make up a picnic.

Fionuala and Aed stood quietly watching her, and when she had disappeared into the kitchen, no doubt to see to the picnic, he turned to his older sister. "What do you think?" he asked.

Fionuala shook her head, her thick dark hair shimmering green in the sunlight. "I don't like it," she said quietly, "it seems so sudden."

Aed nodded in agreement. "I'll tell you what. You go and find Con and Fiac — I'm sure I saw them going into the stables to look at the new ponies — and while you're doing that I'll go and tell Mechar. He will know what to do."

"Tell him to send a messenger bird to Bov's Fort with news to expect us," Fionuala said.

Aed nodded. "That's a good idea." He ran across the courtyard and up the steps towards Mechar's rooms. At least someone would know where they were going. Fionuala stood on the steps for a moment, before turning away towards the stables. For some reason, she was feeling very cold again.

Aife returned with her chariot a little while later. It was driven by one of the servants she had brought with her from her father's court. He took orders only from her and could not — or would not — speak.

Fionuala, Aed, Con and Fiac were waiting by the huge wooden gates of the Fort, and Donn, the charioteer, pulled the chariot around in a tight circle, sending a shower of dust up over the four children as he stopped.

Aife helped them up onto the wood and wicker chariot, and then gave a signal to Donn. He drew back his long whip and cracked it over the horses' heads, and the chariot jolted forward. Donn cracked the whip again, and the four animals picked up speed, and soon they were going as fast as possible, sliding around sharp bends and bouncing over the ruts in the crude road. The four children clung to the sides of the chariot, and soon both Con and Fiac began to look pale and frightened.

Aed touched his step-mother's arm, and shouted above the whipping breeze and the rumble of the hard wooden wheels, "We must stop; my brothers are feeling sick!"

Aife looked at Con and Fiac and nodded. She leaned over and touched Donn on the shoulder and then pointed off to one side, to where the gleam of water could be seen through the trees and bushes. The charioteer immediately pulled on the right hand rein and the horses

veered away from the road and bounced over the hard earth, leaving long tracks in the grass that was still damp from the morning's dew. He drove directly through the bushes, sending startled birds up into the clear blue sky, and disturbing a rabbit which bounded half-way across the field, before it stopped and stood on its hind legs to watch them with button-bright eyes.

The charioteer finally pulled his horses to a halt close to the water's edge. Aed immediately jumped out and helped his two brothers to the ground and then helped Fionuala down. The four of them then walked down onto the small sandy beach beside the water.

"Don't go far," Aife called after them, "we'll picnic here and then we must carry on. I want to reach Bov's Fort by noon."

The four children stood by the water's edge and stared out across the still blue-green waters. Con and Fiac were looking a little better and colour had come back into their cheeks. "He was going so fast," Con complained, "and all that bouncing around was making me feel sick."

"So did I," his twin agreed.

Aife came up behind them, her wooden-soled boots crunching on the sand. "It's such a lovely day," she said, "why don't you go in for a swim; we'll eat when you're finished."

Aed glanced across at Fionuala, and she nodded; there was nothing Aife could do while they were swimming, was there?

They quickly stripped off and dived into the water. It was ice cold and stinging and they gasped with the shock, but luckily the gills in their throats opened and they didn't have to swallow any of the water. They swam easily, like fishes, twisting and turning by using tiny movements of their feet. However, the water was so cold that they soon decided to finish and besides, they were getting hungry.

The four heads broke the surface of the water together. From the distance they looked like seals, sleek and shining. With their arms close by their sides and only their feet moving quickly, they began to swim towards the shore. As they neared the small rough beach they noticed that Aife was nowhere to be seen. They stopped swimming and bobbed in the chill water; where was she? Has she driven off and left them? They hesitated for a few moments, and then Fionuala said, "Well, we can't stay here, can we?" and then she allowed her legs to come to the surface of the water, and she allowed the pull of the water to carry her in to the shore.

They were wading through the shallows when Aife re-appeared. She must have been standing behind a tree watching them, waiting for them to near the shore. The first thing they noticed was that she had changed her clothes, and she was no longer dressed in her gown of green and gold. Now she wore a long gown of midnight black, edged around the throat and hem with broad bands of deep red worked with a strange design in bright gold thread. But what really made the four children stop and stare in fright and curiosity was that she was also wearing a long flowing cloak which glittered and shimmered with strange designs.

And the children of Lir knew that the De Danann only wore these ancient cloaks when they were going to work some strong magic.

Something about the cloak was familiar and then Fionuala suddenly realised what it was. She pointed, her mouth

46

opening into an 'O' of surprise. "That's our father's magical cloak."

Aife strode down the beach in a few quick steps. She was barefoot now and she barely made a sound on the rough sand and pebbles. She smiled, a cold, frightening smile.

"Yes, this is your father's cloak. This cloak is woven from the mists of morning and the dew of evening, from the first shafts of morning sunlight and the last rays of twilight. The foam of the sea-spray and the fresh salt smells have gone into it, and it is made up out of the strength of a sea-storm and the gentleness of a sea-breeze." Aife twirled it about herself, and then held it out with her arms wide. "It is the most powerful magical cloak in these islands."

"Why are you wearing it, step-mother?" Aed asked quietly.

Aife leaned forward and her hard eyes narrowed. "Because I need its strength," she said. "I am going to work the most powerful magic that has ever been worked in Banba."

"And what magic is that?" Fionuala whispered.

Their step-mother took another step forward and smiled coldly. "For far too long you have stood between me and your father; he loves you far more than he loves me. Every time he looks at you, he is reminded of my sister, your mother. So . . . now I am going to remove you," her voice had dropped to a whisper, and the four children had to strain to hear her.

"You cannot kill us," Aed said, "we are the children of Lir, of the tribe of the Tuatha De Danann. If you kill us our ghosts will rise and haunt you."

Aife nodded. "Oh, I know that. No, I am not going to kill

48

you, I am not so foolish." She paused and whirled the shimmering, glittering cloak around her once more. "I am going to change you!"

And before the four children could move, Aife made a strange shape in the air with the fingers of her left hand, and they suddenly found that they were frozen to the spot, unable to move.

Aife then took her time. She first broke a branch off a nearby alder tree and, by using her magical power, changed it into a shining black wand almost half as tall as herself. She then splashed out into the shallows and walked anti-clockwise around the four children with the point of her wand splashing through the water. She then stood back and spoke a *word,* and the circle glowed red and gold on the water. Aife turned back and threw the wand high into the air. The children of Lir saw it shatter into a fine cloud of dust which scattered on the light breeze.

Their step-mother then pulled the magical cloak tightly around her shoulders and bent her head. They could see her forehead creased with strain, and her eyes squeezed tightly shut. Her lips were moving quickly, but no sound came out except a faint buzzing, like an angry bee. And then slowly, slowly, Aife raised her head and opened her eyes. She smiled, showing her sharp pointed teeth and then spread the cloak wide with both arms. The intricate designs began to glow and shine, and soon the entire cloak was a sheet of pulsating light which blinded the four children. And then the light flowed off the cloak and rolled along the ground in a huge ball. It hissed slightly as it moved, and it left behind it a trail of burnt and crisped grass and hardened sand. When it touched the water it exploded into steam which rose up in a thick, dense fog. The children of Lir felt the hot steam tingling along their legs and arms. The tingling quickly increased until it felt like pins and needles, and they found they could no longer feel their feet . . . and then their legs . . . thighs . . . stomachs . . . chests . . . arms . . . necks . . . heads . . .

When they could see again, they found that Aife had grown huge, and towered over them like a giantess. Aed shouted in rage and tried to jump forward. He felt his arms moving, but nothing happened, except that water splashed in every direction. He looked around for his sister and brothers . . . and then he cried aloud in horror and terror.

For Fionuala, Con and Fiac were gone, and in their places three snow-white swans floated on the still waters of the lake. Aed looked down into the water at his own reflection . . . and the small, delicate head of a swan looked back up at him!

Chapter

V

"Our step-mother had changed us into four swans," Fionuala continued, *"and she put a spell on us so that we would remain in the shape of birds for nine hundred years, and even then we would not return to our own shape until we heard the tolling of a church bell. And you must remember that in those days there were no such things as churches or bells in Banba, as Erin was called then.*

"She also put a geas – that is a special sort of spell which made you do something against your will – on us so that we had to spend the first three hundred years on the lake at Derravaragh; the second three hundred in the icy waters of the Straits of Moyle which lies between Banba and Alba, and the final three hundred on the island of Inish Glora off the western coast. To complete the spell, we had to hear the bell of the New God.

"However, even though Aife could rob us of our human forms, she could not take away our voices, and we could still speak perfectly.

"And so we floated there on the cold waters of the lake, feeling the wind ruffling our feathers, and watched our step-mother ride away with her charioteer, and she was laughing . . ."

The chariot had just disappeared over the brow of the hill in a cloud of dust when a single horseman came riding around the bend in the road. He rode slowly, with one hand on the reins, and the other held out before him, holding something which dangled from a string.

The rider paused by the road and then urged his horse across the fields towards the water and the children. He dismounted and pushed his way through the bushes, now following the tracks of the chariot wheels through the tall grass.

The four children of Lir drifted into the tall rushes by the side of the lake and hid there, unsure who it was that had obviously followed them.

The tall, bulky man paused by the water's edge, and brought up his left hand. The four children could see a strange pointed stone turning on the end of a long leather thong. The

53

stone shifted, and then turned to point directly towards the reeds. The tall man stepped closer to the reeds and pushed back the hood of his long grey cloak.

"It's Mechar," Aed said suddenly recognising the figure. He pushed his way out of the reeds and drifted over to their friend.

Mechar frowned when he saw the beautiful snow-white swan drift out of the reeds and move silently towards him. He looked down at the magic stone in his hand: it was now pointing directly towards the swan.

But where were the children?

He had waited until the four of them had gone with Aife before releasing the messenger pigeon and then, when the chariot had rounded the turn in the road, he had set out to follow it. His direction-stone pointed the way, for it was the twin of the stones which he had given Aed and Fionuala, and it would always point in that direction.

And so he was puzzled now. Why did the stone point towards this tall, beautiful swan? The huge bird came up and rubbed its slender head against his hand. Mechar was amazed, for these were usually the shyest of birds. There was a sudden movement in the reeds and then three more swans, one large and two small, moved slowly towards him.

And Mechar suddenly knew!

He fell to his knees in the cold water and looked closely at the four birds. He looked into their clear eyes and he knew them: Aed and Fionuala, Con and Fiac. He knew then what Aife had done, and he knew he had to reach Bov's Fort before she did.

Mechar stroked the bird's heads gently, and there were tears in his eyes. "There is nothing I can do for you now," he whispered, "but I will find your father, and I'll tell Bov what his daughter has done. He should know some way to reverse the spell, I'm sure he will be able to return you to your own bodies."

"I don't think anything can help us now," the tallest swan, Aed, said. "You know that the magic of the Tuatha De Danann is the most powerful magic in the world, and that once made it cannot be undone."

Mechar almost fell backwards with fright. "You can talk!"

"That was something not even Aife could change or take from us," said the second swan, and Mechar recognised Fionuala's voice.

"What will Aife do now?" Aed asked, his feathers rippling across the lake.

"She will probably go on to her father's Fort, and tell them some story about the four of you being kidnapped by bandits, or eaten by wolves." He shrugged. "I'm sure she would make it a very good story." He smiled coldly and stood. "But she does not know that I've sent on a messenger bird, and in the message I've said that I expect her to try and harm you."

"What will you do now?" Aed asked.
"I'm going on to Bov's Fort to tell them what has happened here."

"Bring our father back with you," Con said, with tears in his eyes and a catch in his voice.

"Oh, I will," Mechar promised, "I will".

When Mechar reached Bov's Fort, he found the place in an uproar. He questioned some of the guards and found out that Aife had ridden in earlier, alone and in great distress. She told how she had been on the way to her father's Fort from the White Fort with her four step-children, and her charioteer, Donn. On the way, the children had complained of the heat and so they had stopped at Lake Derravaragh. However, on the beach, the children had been attacked by wild boars — huge pigs with razor-sharp teeth and tusks — and although she and Donn had fought the animals and attempted to save the children, one by one they had been killed and eaten by the boars; Donn had also fallen to their snarling tusks.

Mechar listened in amazement. It was a very clever story, since it meant that there were no bodies to account for, and it also looked as if she were a heroine, who had fought bravely in defence of her step-children. He smiled grimly and wondered what she had done with the charioteer; probably used her magical power to turn him into something — a snail, a moth, a small bird.

He hurried through the Fort, down the long corridors where the guards were rushing to and fro, gathering together a hunting party to go in search of the boars. He found Aife in the throne-room with Bov, her father, and Lir. They all stopped when Mechar strode in through the tall doors without knocking or announcing himself.

Lir took a few steps towards his servant and friend. Mechar could see that the older man was terribly upset and he seemed to have aged suddenly. "You've heard . . ." he began.

Mechar nodded. "I know, my Lord." He paused and added in a loud, angry voice. "I know the truth, my Lord."

Bov looked up at the loud voice. "What do you mean, you know the truth," he demanded, his hard green eyes boring through the younger man.

Mechar looked at him in astonishment. "Didn't you get my message?"

"What message?"

"I sent a carrier-pigeon with a note for you," Mechar said quickly.

Bov nodded. "Aye, I received that message; a strange note saying that you expected my daughter to do the children harm on their journey here." He paused and added in a different tone, glancing across at his daughter, "I ignored it at the time."

Aife looked up in sudden fright. "What nonsense!" she snapped. "I did everything in my power to protect them." Tears came into her eyes and her voice broke, "But the boars were so ferocious . . ."

"Where did the boars attack you?" Mechar asked quietly.

"On the banks of Lake Derravaragh," Aife said quickly. "The children had been swimming, and just as they were coming out of the water, the boars attacked. They must have been waiting in the cover of the bushes." She hung her head again. "My charioteer died defending them."

Mechar took a step forward. "Tell me," he asked quietly, "why didn't you change the wild boars into something else? Your power is transformation; why didn't you use it?"

Lir looked at his wife. "Yes Aife, why didn't you."

Aife looked quickly from Mechar to Lir and then turned to her father. "There was no time; it all happened so quickly."

Bov was looking at her strangely now, and he turned back to Mechar without saying a word to her. "What are you getting at, young man?"

"I have just come from Lake Derravaragh," Mechar said, his voice dropping to a whisper, but which was clearly audible in the great hall. "There are four swans on the waters of the lake; four beautiful, snow-white swans. But these are not ordinary birds, oh no," he shook his head, "for these birds can talk. They are the children of Lir!"

Aife attempted to laugh, but all that came out was a choking sound. She shook her head from side to side. "Oh no, it's not true, it's not true, I never . . ."

Mechar stepped closer to the pale-faced woman. "You used your magical powers to change them into swans," he accused, "and you have placed them under a nine hundred year enchantment."

"It's a lie," Aife screamed. "He hates me, and he's only trying to get me into trouble."

Mechar smiled sadly and shook his head.

Bov called for a servant, and told him to bring the Mirror of Truth. The servant hurried away frightened. He had never seen the king looking so angry before: his hair and beard almost bristled, his face was red, and his eyes were like chips of broken glass in his head.

When the servant returned with the Mirror, he found Aife, Lir's wife, screaming and shouting, first at her husband and then at her father, whilst a third man, whom the servant knew to be one of Lir's personal servants, stood quietly by, a look of terrible sorrow on his broad face.

58

Bov took the magic mirror and dismissed the servant. He carefully removed the black and red silk cloth that covered the mirror, and then held the glass up in front of Aife. It was quite big, almost as large as a shield, with a beautiful, intricately designed golden frame. But the glass itself was black: it reflected nothing.

"Look into the mirror, daughter," Bov commanded, "and tell me once again what happened. Remember," he warned her, "this is the Mirror of Truth, you cannot lie to it."

Aife began her story once again, and as she spoke a picture formed in the black glass. But it was not a picture of the children being attacked by a pack of wild boar, rather it was the image of Aife standing by the water's edge dressed in her magical cloak and using her spells to transform the children into four swans. It showed her riding away with Donn, and then it showed her changing the charioteer into a tiny, rainbow-winged fly as they neared Bov's Fort.

Bov's anger was frightening. He had loved his grandchildren dearly, and was horrified to think that his daughter, their step-mother, could do such a terrible thing to them. He turned away from her without saying a word, and walked to his throne. He picked up the crown and sceptre that lay across the beautifully carved stone seat and sat down. He put the high golden crown on his red hair and then lifted the sceptre high. He spoke an ancient word and the length of beaten gold turned into a plain wooden wand.

"You have done a terrible thing, my daughter," he said coldly, pointing the wand at her. "You have shamed me and this noble house, and by doing so, you have shamed all the people of the Tuatha De Danann. You are no longer welcome in my house, and no longer can you be part of the People of the Goddess." He began to move the wand in a strange pattern in the air.

"You have taken away my grand-children's human form, and so I too will take away your form."

Bov moved the wand again and a sudden cold breeze blew through the throne room. Aife began to shiver, although neither Lir nor Mechar felt the intense cold she was obviously feeling. A thin covering of ice formed on her hair and eyelashes, and her pale green-tinged skin turned blue with the cold. Soon a pale thin covering of ice clothed her, and then it gradually began to thicken and soon Aife could no longer be seen within the solid block of ice.

Bov then spoke a word, and a thin line of bright green fire shot from the tip of the wand and darted towards the block of ice. It struck the surface and then shot to and fro, darting and spinning and wherever it touched the ice began to melt. The green fire spun once around the ice block and then darted back to the wand.

The three men then stood silently waiting for the ice to melt. And when it did Aife was gone!

Lir stepped forward into the spreading pool and poked

amongst the lumps of half-frozen ice and then he pulled out a small, long-tailed, shining-eyed lizard. The creature opened its mouth and hissed, and a forked tongue flickered back and forth. It hissed again and then unfolded a pair of almost transparent wings and flapped upwards. It circled once around the small silent group, hissing all the time, and then headed out through the open window.

Aife had received her just reward.

Chapter
VI

"And so we began the first three hundred years of our enchantment on the cold waters of Lough Derravaragh. Oh, our father and grandfather and the greatest wizards and magicians in all the known world came and tried to turn us back into our human form, but no-one succeeded. It turned out that Aife had set that spell in a certain way, a way that only she could undo, and so we were trapped.

"Our father moved his court to the banks of the lake, and the greatest scholars and teachers in the world came and taught us. We learned many things, but most of all, we learned to sing. And soon our music and songs became known through the length and breadth of Banba. People came from miles around just to hear us sing and if we sang sad songs, nearly everybody cried, but if we sang happy songs, then everyone laughed and smiled.

"But the first three hundred years soon passed. We did not feel the time slipping by, and it was only when we came to say goodbye to our father on the last morning did we actually realise just how long we had spent on the waters of the lake . . ."

Lir had grown old as he lived by the waters of Lough Derravaragh. His green hair was now streaked with silver and there were lines on his forehead and about his eyes. He stood on the sandy beach and watched the four swans — his children — glide silently across the water towards him. He shaded his eyes and squinted into the morning mist which clung to the water, trying to distinguish them. At one time, when he was younger, and his sight clearer than it was now, he would have been able to tell one from the other even from the other side of the lake. But now . . . he smiled sadly; he would soon have to rest in the long sleep of the De Danann. Lir's old eyes filled with tears as he recognised the larger swan. "My son," he said in a whisper.

"Father . . ." Aed bowed his long slender neck, but could not speak.

A second swan joined them, and Lir recognised Fionuala's bright eyes even before he heard her sweet voice. "Father," she began, "we must leave this lake today; the first part of the enchantment is over, and now we must head north to the wild waters of Moyle."

The old king nodded. "I know," he said. "I have watched the years come and go. I have watched my friends and servants grow old and tired and go into the secret resting places of the De Danann — soon I will follow them." He paused and shook his head sadly. "Soon my children, there will be no De Danann left in Banba, for we will all have retired to the secret places. It will be many years before we come again." There were tears in his eyes again as he looked across the cold misty waters of the lake. "When you go now I will be alone," he said.

"You will have Mechar," Aed said.

Lir shook his head. "Mechar fell into the long sleep last night," he whispered. "There is no-one left here but me."

"Father," Fionuala said quietly, feeling the strong pull of the curse, "we must go now."

Lir nodded and then, as each swan came up to him, he bent and kissed the top of its silken head. The four swans then drifted out into the centre of the lake, until they were almost lost in the fog, and then they flapped their huge wings and began to beat their way across the water. The morning mists billowed and curled about them like smoke and then they were up into the air, their wings beating strongly. They strung out in a line, with Fionuala in the lead, Aed behind and Con and Fiac following, and then swung around in a circle over the lake. They sang an ancient song of parting, full of sorrow and heartbreak, and anyone who heard it felt the tears come to their eyes, and even the birds and animals fell silent as the haunting music filled the air.

The four swans then turned towards the north and, with

the wind in their faces, they set out for the Straits of Moyle. And the last they ever saw of their father was a sad old man standing tall and proud by the waters of Lough Derravaragh with tears on his face.

The four swans flew northwards for most of the morning. They flew over lakes and rivers, mountains and huge forests — for most of the land was covered with trees in those days. Once or twice they passed the shining towers of a De Danann fort, and they saw the tall figures standing on the battlements waving up at them, for everyone in Banba knew the children of Lir: they had become a legend in their own lifetime.

About noon they passed over the barren northern cliffs and soon they were out over the Straits of Moyle where they would spend the second stage of their nine hundred year enchantment. They dropped downwards onto the grey sea and settled on a barren clump of rock, exhausted after their long flight.

All around them there was nothing but a flat expanse of cold, grey-green sea. The water was icy, and there were even tiny chunks of ice which had floated down from the frozen northern seas. A chill wind blew down from the north and occasionally a stronger gust blew rain and sleet in on the four shivering birds.

They remained on the tiny rock all day, while all around them the wind and sea rose and low dark clouds rolled across the angry sky.

"There's a storm coming," Aed said, shouting above the howling of the wind.

"The first of many I should think," Fionuala said.

"What will we do?" Aed asked, sounding worried.

67

"We must try and stay together," Fionuala replied. "We'll make this rock our base, and if the storm separates us, we must try and return to it . . ."

She had barely finished speaking when a huge wave washed in over the barren rock, and when it had passed, the four swans were gone, swept away into the wild and stormy sea.

The storm lasted nearly three days. It rained snow and ice, and the wind blowing down from the arctic north was as sharp as a knife and bitterly cold. Thunder and lightning rolled across the skies and the lightning flashes turned the night into day.

The four swans were roughly tossed about in all directions. Fionuala and Aed managed to stay together for a little while, and once they passed very close to another white swan which could have been Con, although the bird had come and gone so quickly it was hard to tell. However, after a terrific peal of thunder and a jagged streak of lightning, Fionuala and Aed became separated, and now the four swans were alone on the wild waves.

Fionuala was the first to reach the barren clump of rock they had chosen to be their base. She was bruised and battered, cold and terrible hungry. She was also very tired, but the first thing she did was to climb to the highest point of the small clump of rock and look about her in every direction for her missing brothers. But the grey sea was deserted.

She remained there for the rest of the morning, watching and waiting. The sea was a little calmer, although the occasional wave still washed over the rock and she had to struggle to keep her footing. But the storm was over — although to the far south there were still grey clouds, and

THE SONG OF THE CHILDREN OF LIR

she guessed it would be raining now over Banba.

As the day wore on she began to sing. She sang in her strong clear voice that carried out over the waves in every direction. She sang the songs she had learned as a child; she sang the songs she and Aed had sung to each other; she sang the songs they had both taught to the twins, and she sang of the Tuatha De Danann, the People of the Goddess.

And as the day drifted into evening and the sun was slipping down in the sky, she began to despair of ever seeing her brothers again. And for a single moment her voice broke and she stopped singing . . .

And in the silence she heard the high sweet sound of music. She raised her head and looked in all directions, and there, on the eastern horizon, were two white specks. Fionuala sang again, and this time she sang with joy as she watched Aed and Con swim towards her.

But of Fiac, there was no sign.

Both of her brothers had their own stories to tell; of being thrown far and wide, battered and almost drowned, caught and pulled, pushed and twisted by the wind and water until they didn't know where they were. But they had found their way back by following the sound of her voice.

And then the three of them sang together, hoping to call their missing brother to them, but although they sang late into the night, there was no sign of him, and so, one by one, they fell into an exhausted sleep.

That night Fionuala had a dream. She dreamt that she was back in the hidden blue room where her father had shown her and Aed their sleeping mother. And in her dream she saw her mother open her eyes and sit up on her coral bed. She stood gracefully, her long gown of pale green silk whispering

70

about her as it settled, and then she took Fionuala's hand. Together they walked from the smaller room into the larger, circular chamber and, with her small, beautiful hand she pointed to the wall. In her dream Fionuala could see that it was no longer painted blue, and now it showed a picture of the small clump of rock and the three sleeping swans painted in dark blues and purples. Eva's finger moved and pointed to another part of the wall and there, not too far from the others, was the picture of a small battered and bleeding swan floating on a moonlit sea.

Fionuala opened her eyes and looked around in confusion, wondering where she was. She shook her head, trying to clear the images of her dreams which had been so real.

And then, as if from a great distance, she remembered her father's words when he had shown Aed and herself their mother, *". . . she will be watching over you . . . and if you are ever in any great danger . . . she will be there . . ."*

Fionuala immediately awakened her brothers and, although they were unsure whether to believe her or not, they followed behind as she set out across the waves in the direction she had been shown in her dream. And, just as Aed was about to say, "This is a waste of time . . ." they came upon Fiac, bruised and battered, but alive, just as Fionuala had been shown in her dream.

And so the Children of Lir were re-united.

Chapter VII

THE SONG OF THE CHILDREN OF LIR

"The three hundred years we spent in the seas of the Strait of Moyle were the hardest of our enchantment. It was a terrible place. We were always cold, wet and hungry, and sometimes it got so cold that the sea froze in a solid sheet all around us, and the skin of our feet stuck fast to the icy rock.

"During those times we sang the old songs of our people, for the sounds of our voices would crack the ice and calm the wind. You see, there was a magic in our music.

"But everything must come to an end and eventually the second three hundred years passed. We had no way of knowing the time, except that we saw the stars moving through the sky and we could tell the passing seasons by the length of the day and the height of the sun and moon.

"And so one morning I woke up and I knew – I just knew – that the second three hundred years had passed, and we were now forced to move on. I woke my brothers . . ."

The four swans flapped
their huge wings, making
little ripples on the icy water
and then slowly, one by one,
they rose into the chill morning air.
   The sun had not quite risen and the
sky to the east was ablaze with different
colours, mostly shades of red and gold, and
the low fleecy clouds were touched with pink.
   The four children turned to the south and once
again they flew over the island of Banba. Almost
immediately they noticed changes. Where once the
great forests had grown, there were now small
collections of houses and some-
times large castles. The
long straight lines of roads
were everywhere. Along the coasts
the towns were larger and there were
many tall-masted ships anchored in the harbours.
And it suddenly made them realise just how much time
they had actually spent as swans: six hundred years!

On their way over the country they changed direction slightly and flew south, looking for their old home. They flew over Lough Derravaragh where they had spent the first three hundred years and while at the time it had seemed so large, it now looked so small. They flew above where the White Fort should have been, but there was nothing there now; the Fort with the shining towers and its roof of beaten gold was gone and in its place was a low grass mound with bushes and trees growing on it. And the children of Lir wept then, for they knew that the age of the Tuatha De Danann was gone, and with them, a lot of the magic had gone out of this world.

They turned away then and headed west for Inish Glora. It was evening before they reached the island, and the sun was sinking down into the sea in a magnificent sunset of brilliant reds, golds, pinks and even a touch of blue and green.

Inish Glora was a tiny island off the western coast of Banba. It was uninhabited except for a small colony of seals and hundreds of seabirds of all shapes and sizes, and there wasn't a rock on the island that wasn't touched with white streaks.

The four swans found a tiny nook under the cliffs and soon fell into an exhausted sleep.

They awoke to hear the howling of the wind whipping in off the Western Ocean and the pounding of the waves on the rocky beach: there was a storm brewing.

The storm, which broke around noon brought back terrible memories of the time they had spent in the Straits of Moyle, and they wondered were they doomed to spend another miserable three hundred years cold and wet and hungry. Was there to be no peace for them?

However, the storm soon passed overhead and rolled in

across the mainland, and they could hear the thunder booming and the lightning cracking long into the night, and it wasn't until close to morning before the three boys fell into an uneasy sleep.

Fionuala waited until she was sure that they were asleep before she took to the air and flew the short distance to the mainland. She was looking for shelter of some sort; the summer was almost over and soon the winter storms would come crashing in over the island, and she knew that they could not survive another three hundred winters like the last three hundred.

The shoreline along this part of the coast was very rough, with many cliffs and caves and rocky beaches, and she soon found what she was looking for: a large dry cave, but which had a tiny opening. The opening was big enough to allow the swans in, but not so big that it couldn't be blocked up from the inside to keep out the wind and rain.

When she returned to the island, she found her brothers awake and worried. They had been about to go in search of her.

"We didn't know where you had gone," Aed said.

"I am sorry," she said, "but I thought I would be back before you had woken up."

"Where have you been?" Con asked.

Fionuala pointed with one long-feathered wing towards the mainland. "I was over there looking for a better place for us to spend the next three hundred years."

"But we have to spend all our time here on Inish Glora," Fiac said.

The tall swan shook her small head gracefully. "When our step-mother cursed us, she said that we must spend our time in the waters *about* Inish Glora." She pointed towards the mainland again. "Those waters are about Inish Glora."

"So there is nothing stopping us from settling there?" Con asked.

Fionuala shook her head. "Nothing."

And so they settled on the mainland in the cave that Fionuala had found, and they spent the first few weeks there, warm and dry for the first time in over three hundred years.

And then one morning Con and Fiac, who had gone flying in over the mainland, returned tremendously excited.

The two large birds extended their huge wings and settled down onto the beach in a shower of sand. Aed and Fionuala came running, thinking something was wrong.

"You must come," Con said breathlessly, before they could say anything.

"Oh, it's perfect," his twin agreed, "just perfect."

And so, a little puzzled and amused, Aed and Fionuala followed their younger brothers as they flew above the cliffs and a short distance inland. The twins swung around to the south and then dipped down, and there below them was a beautiful sheltered lake. It was a saltwater lake, and so it didn't break their geas, since it was the same water that washed over Inish Glora, and it was surrounded on three sides by trees and bushes and on the fourth by a small green field.

It was perfect and so they settled there.

In the evenings as the sun was setting in the Western Ocean, they would sing together, and then the birds of the air and the birds of the sea would gather on the branches of the trees, in the bushes and on the water and listen spellbound to the four beautifully blended voices, and in time that small lake became known as the Lake of Birds.

Time passed slowly for the four children of Lir, and to measure the passing days, they would take a small round stone from the beach and place it by the side of the lake, one stone for each day. Now, when this pile had grown quite large, an old man came and settled down at the side of their lake.

79

He was small and frail, with long grey hair and an equally long grey beard, and he moved slowly, leaning on a tall stick.

The first thing he did when he came to the lake was to start building a small round hut at the eastern end of the lake in the small field. Early every morning he would go down to the beach and, with a thick piece of rope, he would drag the stones up along the beach, up the steep path and across the field to the side of the lake. He would then place the stones one on top of the other and use wet clay to cement them together.

But sometimes the larger blocks would be too heavy for the old man and he would fall into an exhausted sleep on the ground beside them, after praying to God to help him.

And in the morning he would find the stone in place.

What the old man didn't know was that while he slept the four swans would each take one end of the rope and, by using the powerful wings, lift the stone into place.

The children watched the old man curiously. He was the first human they had seen since they last saw their father all those years ago, and Fionuala said that he reminded her of the Druids, the holy men when she was a child. Con then wanted to know what sort of holy man he was, because the Druids usually wore long white robes and carried little golden sickles and wore crowns of holly and oak.

Fionuala was quiet for a long time after that and then she said, very quietly, and with such a strange note in her voice that her brothers looked at her. "Do you remember when our step-mother put her curse on us, she said that we would not be released until the bell of the New God was heard in the land?"

Aed looked across at the old man. "Do you think he is a follower of this new god?"

"I don't know," Fionuala said, "should we ask him?"

And so the four swans drifted across the waters of the lake and in towards the old man who was plastering his little hut with a thick covering of mud. When this dried in the sun it would make the hut draught-proof.

They waited in the water until he had finished, and then he came down and knelt in the shallow water to wash the mud and clay off his hands. He smiled at the four swans.

"Well, how are you today? I'm afraid I've no bread for you, but I'm going to make some tomorrow, and you will have some then." When the old man made bread — short, flat loaves — he usually gave some to the swans.

"That would be very nice, thank you," Fionuala said quietly.

The old man jumped backwards in fright and landed with a splash in the water. He sat there looking at the swans in amazement.

Had one of them just spoken to him?

"I'm sorry if I frightened you," Fionuala said, drifting closer.

The old man scrambled backwards out of the water, and then he moved his right hand up and across in a strange gesture and spoke in a foreign language. He then stood as if he were waiting for something to happen — almost as if he expected the four swans to disappear in a puff of smoke.

"Oh," he said when nothing happened, "you are real."

"Of course," Aed said, coming in closer, "what did you expect?"

"You can both talk," he said in astonishment.

"We all talk," the swan with the girl's voice said. "My name is Fionuala, and these are my brothers, Aed, Con and Fiac."

"Talking swans," the old man said, and then his sharp eyes lit up with delight and understanding. "Of course, the children of Lir!"

"You know about us?" Aed asked.

"But of course; all Erin knows the legend of the children of Lir."

"A legend?" Con asked.

The old man nodded. "Aye, a legend; you and all your magical race have long passed into legend." He shook his head sadly, and then, suddenly remembering, he said, "My name is Mochua."

"Are you a holy man?" Fiac asked.

Mochua nodded. "I am a follower of Our Lord Jesus Christ," he said, and made the same crossing sign in the air.

"Tell us about that Christ," Fionuala said. "When our step-mother enchanted us, she said we would not be released until the bell of the New God was heard in our land."

83

THE SONG OF THE CHILDREN OF LIR

And so Mochua sat down by the side of the lake and spoke to the children of Lir about the birth and life of Jesus, and he spoke of the followers of Christ and of Patrick, who had carried the Word to Erin, and whose follower Mochua was.

VIII

"My story is nearly done now," Fionuala said, *"and only a little remains to be told.*

"We stayed with Mochua the Holy for many years. He read to us from his holy books and we listened to the Word of God, and in return we sang in the tiny church he had built and people came from miles around just to listen to us, and they said that we had the voices of angels.

"At that time Mochua was collecting pieces of metal, and the people would bring him old swords and shields, arrowheads and the rusted tops of spears, and he gave them to the local blacksmith who used them to make a bell. We were very excited about this of course, for when Mochua sounded the bell, then we would change back into our human forms.

"But on the day the bell was installed, a terrible thing happened.

"We had all gathered in the small church early one morning, and Mochua was going to say some prayers over the beautifully carved bell, when there was a rattling of metal, shouts and the sound of horses' hooves outside . . ."

A tall shadow darkened the doorway of the tiny church.
Mochua looked up from the altar and then opened his mouth
in surprise as a warrior dressed in armour and a long flowing
cloak stepped into the small circular building. He had a long
sword in his hand, and his head was covered in a horned
helmet.

"What do you want?" Mochua demanded.

The warrior nodded towards the four swans that were

sitting to one side of the small stone altar. "Them," he said.

"No!" the old priest shouted, and then he added in a quieter voice, "How dare you come into the House of God with a sword in your hand and without removing your helmet."

The warrior took one step forward, and lifted up his sword. The light from the candles reflected off it, turning it into a shining bar of gold. "I am Lairgren," he said coldly. "I am the King of Connaught, and I have promised these singing swans to my wife Dessa, the princess of Munster."

"You cannot have them," Mochua said, and stood in front of the swans.

"If you try and stop me old man," the king said loudly, "I will pull your church down and throw the stones in the lake."

Fionuala took a few steps forward. "Don't worry," she said to the old priest, "we will go with him."

Lairgren was startled when he heard the swan speaking with the young girl's voice; it was true then, up to now he had not actually believed the stories. He called in four of his men and they each took one of the birds and carried them outside where they had a chariot waiting.

But they were barely outside the doors of the church when a bell began to toll, its high, sweet notes ringing across the waters of the lake and echoing off the stones.

For a single moment everything seemed to freeze, and then the four men carrying the swans dropped their bundles with shouts of horror. A sudden breeze had blown up and swept across the waters of the lake, gathering up the mist that still clung to it into a solid ball, sweeping in over the land and covering the four swans. The ball of grey-white mist grew and was abruptly coloured with long streaks and dashes of colour. Tiny bubbles gathered and burst with all the colours of the rainbow. The four swans were completely hidden now behind a solid wall of mist which quickly changed colour — green, blue, yellow and then back to blue again. There was a strange smell in the air, like the smell of fish, salt and seaweed when the tide goes out. And then the magical breeze blew again and slowly, slowly the mist began to disperse in a light blue cloud.

The swans were gone. In their places stood four small figures; three pale-skinned men and one delicately beautiful woman. The woman stepped forward and smiled. "We are the children of Lir," she said, her voice as sweet as a song.

"And so we changed back into our human forms," Fionuala said. "When Lairgren saw us, he grew frightened and rode away with his men, and we never saw him again. We were baptised that same day by Mochua, and we became followers of Christ.

"That was many years ago now. Mochua is gone, and the world is changing quickly, but we remain, and here we will remain until that day when we too must go into the world beyond . . ."

Her story finished, the old woman stood stiffly and pressed her tiny webbed hands against the small of her back.

She said goodnight to each of the children and then stood by the apple tree and watched the older children take the younger ones home to the lights of the small town that were twinkling in the distance. The children always stopped at the turn in the road and waved back at her, and she always waited for them to get that far before she turned away and made her way towards the church.

It had grown since that time when she had first seen it. Priests and holy men and sometimes even kings had come and added bits and pieces to it and it was now quite large. But Fionuala always went to a little side chapel — which had been the original building — where she would usually find Aed, Con and Fiac waiting for her. And they would pray there for a little while before retiring for the night to their little house nearby.

And if anyone had been watching them walk from the church to their house in the light of the full moon, he would have seen that they cast no shadows . . .

For they were the last of the magical Tuatha De Danann. They were the Children of Lir.

Our song is sung
Our tale is told,
The song of the
Children of Lir is done,
But the magic lingers on.